Fancy

Fancy

By Kristin Earhart

Illustrated by Elisabeth Alba

SCHOLASTIC INC.

New York   Toronto   London   Auckland
Sydney   Mexico City   New Delhi   Hong Kong

To Leslie and the original Fancy.
And to Lyndsi, and all the barn memories still to come.
−K.J.E.

For Noonie and Joe.
−E. A.

Library of Congress Cataloging-in-Publication Data is available.

ISBN 978-0-545-12098-2

Copyright © 2010 by Reeves International, Inc.
All rights reserved. Published by Scholastic Inc.
BREYER, STABLEMATES, and BREYER logos are trademarks
and/or registered trademarks of Reeves International, Inc.
SCHOLASTIC, CARTWHEEL BOOKS, and associated logos are trademarks
and/or registered trademarks of Scholastic Inc.

10 9 8 7 6 5 4 3 2 1   10 11 12 13 14/0

Printed in Singapore   46
First printing, September 2010

Table of Contents

The Stables at Windy Lane

Today, Grace was starting riding lessons. She had been to Windy Lane Stables many times. Her big brother, Owen, took riding lessons there.

Leah was Owen's riding trainer. Now she was Grace's trainer, too. Leah waved to Grace and Owen.

"Grace, I'm so glad you are here for lessons," said Leah. "You'll love riding. I'm sure of it."

Grace had never ridden a horse before.
She was excited—and scared.

"I'm going to get Copper ready," Owen
said. He grabbed a bucket of brushes. Then
he rushed off to the Quarter Horse's stall.

"Let's go meet Fancy," Leah said to
Grace. "You will ride her for lessons."

They walked up to a stall. Grace peeked
over the stall door.

Fancy had twinkling brown eyes. She
also had big spots of mud on her gray coat.
For a pony named Fancy, she was very dirty!

"Fancy, you need to be brushed and
groomed!" Leah said with a laugh. "Fancy
just loves the mud." Leah smiled at Grace.
The trainer walked into Fancy's stall and
put on her halter.

"Let Fancy smell your hand," said Leah.

Grace gently held out her hand. Fancy stepped forward and sniffed.

"It tickles!" Grace laughed.

Fancy was a small pony, but she still looked big to Grace! Grace took a deep breath. Could she trust Fancy?

Just then, the pony turned to Grace. Fancy nuzzled Grace's pockets with her soft, pink nose, looking for treats. Grace had to smile.

Chapter 2

Getting Ready

"Once Fancy is clean, I'll teach you how to put on the saddle and bridle," said Leah.

Grace saw the mud on Fancy's gray coat. She saw the knots in Fancy's mane and tail.

"Let's clean the mud off, brush out those knots, and pick out her feet," said Leah. "Fancy is a Welsh pony," Leah told Grace. "She is very smart."

"I will help you get Fancy ready today,"
Leah said. "After a few lessons, you will do it
by yourself."

Grace nodded. She had a lot to learn.

Owen stopped by to check on Grace.

"Let's put on the saddle now," Leah said. Grace found the saddle on the rack by Fancy's stall. It was heavy!

"I'll help you, sis," said Owen.

Grace and Owen lifted the saddle up high.

"Nice and easy," Leah directed, but Grace lost her grip! The saddle flopped down on Fancy's back.

"Did I hurt her?" Grace asked.

"She's pretty tough," said Leah with a smile. "You will get the hang of it. It just takes practice."

"I'm sorry, Fancy," Grace said softly.

Next Leah showed Grace how to fasten the saddle.

"The girth is like a belt," Leah explained. "It goes under Fancy's belly. It stops the saddle from sliding off."

Then Leah helped Grace put on the bridle. The bridle had reins. "The rider uses the reins to tell the horse what to do," Leah said. At last Grace was ready to ride.

In the Saddle

Grace enjoyed her time at the Windy Lane Stables.

Each week, she raced into the barn. She could not wait to see Fancy.

When Fancy saw Grace, the pretty pony nickered. Fancy's eyes were always bright, but her coat was always dirty.

"Not again," Grace would say, laughing. "You don't look very fancy to me." Then she brushed the brown spots out of the pony's coat.

Grace loved riding. She especially loved riding Fancy. Fancy was slow, steady, and very careful—just like Grace.

Grace had been practicing, and she had learned a lot. She could put the saddle on Fancy's back. She could put the bridle on Fancy's head. She could use the reins to tell Fancy where to go.

There was still one thing Grace could not do. She could not pull herself into the saddle. She tried to get on Fancy every week, but she could not do it by herself.

It was a brisk fall day. Grace and Owen had a lesson with a group of riders. Grace led Fancy into the ring. She saw Owen on Copper and waved.

Leah came over to Grace. It was time to get on.

"Okay, just like we practiced,"
Leah said. "Put your foot in the stirrup,
hold on to Fancy's mane, and pull
yourself up."

Grace tried but she could not reach the stirrup.

"Let's use the step stool again," Leah said.

Grace sighed. She climbed the stool. She put her foot in the stirrup. She swung her other leg over the saddle, and she was on.

During the lesson, the other horses were faster than Fancy. Grace watched them pass, but she did not mind. She liked Fancy's slow, steady trot.

At the end of the lesson, Leah spoke to the riders. "The barn is having a small show next week," she announced. "There will be some jumping classes and games. I hope you can come."

Grace's heart jumped. She wanted to ride Fancy in the show.

"You just started lessons," Leah said to Grace. "But there is a class you can enter. It's called Saddle Up and Go!"

"It's a race," Owen said. "You have to tack up, get on the pony, and trot to the finish line."

"You can even use the step stool," Leah offered.

"But you have to be fast," said Owen.

Leah laughed. "Oh, Owen," she said in a kind voice, "it's just for fun."

Grace smiled at her trainer and gave Fancy a pat. Grace usually did not like to go fast, but she did want a blue ribbon.

The Fast Track

On the day of the show, Grace and Owen came early. Saddle Up and Go was the last class, but Grace wanted to see everything. When she got to Fancy's stall, she looked inside. "Fancy, you're a mess!"

The pony nickered and nuzzled Grace's pocket for a treat.

After Grace brushed Fancy, she watched the older riders. Everyone rode well. The winners received ribbons. They were pretty and bright.

It was finally time for Saddle Up and Go. Grace led Fancy to the ring. "We can do it," she told Fancy. "We can be fast."

The riders and ponies stood at the starting line. All the equipment was sitting on the ground waiting for them.

Leah blew a whistle. The race began! Grace quickly put Fancy's bridle on her, then picked up the saddle. She ran back and slid it onto Fancy's back. She pulled the girth tight.

Next Grace had to get in the saddle. She looked around. The step stool was not there! Grace took a deep breath. She lifted her foot and put it in the stirrup. She grabbed Fancy's mane and the front of the saddle. Then she hopped twice and pulled herself up.

Grace swung her leg over the saddle, and it hit Fancy's side with a thump. Fancy took off!

"Go!" Grace called. Fancy trotted toward the finish line. Grace held on tight. The finish line came closer. Fancy crossed it first!

Everyone was happy for Grace and Fancy.

"Way to go!" Owen cheered.

"I have never seen Fancy go so fast," said one of the riders.

"Nice work," agreed Leah.

"We really are a good team," Grace said to Fancy. She put the blue ribbon on the pony's bridle and smiled.

"There you go, girl. You can't get fancier than that!"

About the Pony

Facts about Welsh Ponies:

1. Welsh ponies originally came from the hills of Wales, a division of the United Kingdom on the western border of England.

2. There are four types of Welsh ponies: Welsh mountain ponies, Welsh pony of cob type, Welsh cob, and the Welsh part-breed.

3. Welsh ponies are known for their loyalty and gentle disposition, which makes this breed perfect for first-time riders.

4. The Welsh pony has large friendly eyes and a small pretty head. They have strong backs and legs. They are good jumpers and are good at pulling wagons and carts.

5. The average Welsh pony is 12.2 hands high, which means it is only forty-nine inches high at the shoulders.